P

AUS:

Crocodile
Jack

Jack can't believe that Tom is asking
him to go fishing. Tom never wants
his little brother around, ever!
But this time Tom needs Jack.
He wants him to keep a lookout
for crocodiles . . .

Tick the
Aussie Bites
<u>you</u> have read!

☐ **CROCODILE JACK**
Leonie Norrington
Illustrated by Terry Denton

☐ **HAGGIS McGREGOR AND THE NIGHT OF THE SKULL MOON**
Jen Storer
Illustrated by Gus Gordon

☐ **THE BAKED BEAN BANDIT**
Simon Mitchell
Illustrated by Gus Gordon

☐ **A CHOOK CALLED HARRY**
Phillip Gwynne
Illustrated by Terry Denton

☐ **MOON STATION**
Rachel Flynn
Illustrated by Judy Watson

☐ **FOOL'S GOLD**
Margaret Clark
Illustrated by Andrew McLean

Aussie Bites

Crocodile Jack

Leonie Norrington

Illustrated by Terry Denton

Puffin Books

For my Luke. L.N.
For Roza Aharon. T.D.

PUFFIN BOOKS

Published by the Penguin Group
Penguin Group (Australia)
250 Camberwell Road
Camberwell, Victoria 3124, Australia
(a division of Pearson Australia Group Pty Ltd)
Penguin Group (USA) Inc.
375 Hudson Street, New York, New York 10014, USA
Penguin Group (Canada)
90 Eglinton Avenue East, Suite 700,
Toronto ON M4P 2Y3, Canada
(a division of Pearson Penguin Canada Inc.)
Penguin Books Ltd
80 Strand, London WC2R 0RL, England
Penguin Ireland
25 St Stephen's Green, Dublin 2, Ireland
(a division of Penguin Books Ltd)
Penguin Books India Pvt Ltd
11, Community Centre, Panchsheel Park, New Delhi -110 017, India
Penguin Group (NZ)
67 Apollo Drive, Rosedale, Auckland 0632, New Zealand
(a division of Pearson New Zealand Ltd)
Penguin Books (South Africa) (Pty) Ltd
24 Sturdee Avenue, Rosebank, Johannesburg 2196, South Africa

Penguin Books Ltd, Registered Offices: 80 Strand, London WC2R 0RL, England

First published by Pearson Education Australia, 2004
Published in this revised edition by Penguin Group (Australia), 2011

1 3 5 7 9 10 8 6 4 2

Text copyright © Leonie Norrington 2004
Illustrations copyright © Terry Denton, 2011

The moral right of the author and illustrator has been asserted.

Text and cover design by Karen Scott © Penguin Group (Australia)
Series designed by Cameron Midson, based on an original series design by Ruth Grüner
Typeset in New Century Schoolbook by Post Pre-press Group, Brisbane, Queensland
Printed and bound in Australia by McPherson's Printing Group, Maryborough, Victoria

National Library of Australia
Cataloguing-in-Publication data:
Norrington, Leonie.
Crocodile Jack / Leonie Norrington; illustrated by
Terry Denton.
ISBN 9780143305958 (pbk.)
Aussie bites.
Crocodiles – Juvenile fiction.
Denton, Terry, 1950 - .

A823.3

puffin.com.au

Chapter One

'Jack! We're going fishing. You want
to come?'

Jack can't believe his ears. His
big brother Tom is asking him to go
fishing! Tom goes everywhere with
his mate Xavier. They never let Jack
go with them, ever. Once, when Jack
followed them, they even hid behind a
tree. When he came close they jumped
out and yelled, 'Rack off, you midget!'

Now Tom's asking him straight out,
'Well, you wanna come or what?'

Jack says, 'Yes, please!'

'Okay, you climb through the shed window and get a lure out of Dad's tackle box. You're small enough to get through.'

'But that's stealing.'

'No, it's not! We'll put it back as soon as we're finished. Get the orange-and-yellow Vibra Tail.'

'Why don't you just ask Dad?'

'I did!' Tom says. 'He said no. He reckons the water's too high and there's still too many crocs around.' Tom makes a face as if Dad's totally stupid. Then he says, 'Come on, Jack. You gonna do it? Or are you just a scaredy cat!'

'I'm not scared!' Jack says,

swallowing the guilty feeling tickling
his belly. He climbs in through the
shed window, and before he can think,
he is outside again, giving Tom the
lure. And he's running with Tom and

3

Xavier down past the cattle yards and along the track to the creek.

Suddenly Tom stops, so fast that Jack nearly slams into his back. There's Nanna Clara, Xavier's grandmother, sitting on the bank with Xavier's cousin Mareeta. They're fishing. The boys can hear the rest of the kids playing on the sandbar with Xavier's grandad. Jack lifts his hand, ready to yell out, to say hello. Tom grabs him and puts his finger up to his mouth to say, *Be quiet*. Then they go back up the track and walk carefully through the bush – the long way round, so Nanna Clara won't see them.

That's weird, Jack thinks. *Nanna Clara*

knows all the best places for fishing. She knows where to find turtle, yabbies, perch or barramundi. If Tom and Xavier want to go fishing, they should have asked her.

But he doesn't say anything. He's just happy to be allowed to go with the older boys, so he keeps quiet and follows them.

Chapter Two

The creek is still high and running fast. Creamy water, thick with silt, swirls around the tree trunks. Every year, in the Wet season, all the little creeks swell up and spread across the land until it looks like a great flat mirror. While the water is high, massive saltwater crocodiles swim upstream looking for food. They stay there for months, hunting. They don't go back to the big rivers and the sea until the creeks are clear and shallow, and there isn't enough water to hide them.

Jack can see the water is still high
enough for a big crocodile to live there.
It's so murky, he thinks, *you couldn't see
a whale under the water, let alone a croc.*

It's hard to find a good clear fishing

spot. Overhanging trees with tangled vines looping between them crowd the bank. There's nowhere the boys can cast their lines without getting them hooked up in the branches. They walk and walk until, 'This is a good place,' Tom says. He starts climbing out along the trunk of a big tree that has fallen across the water.

'Hey, don't go there!' Jack yells. 'Tom! There could be a big croc!'

Tom laughs. 'Don't panic, little brother. She'll be right. The crocs are heading back to sea now.'

'But there's still heaps of water.'

'Yeah, and heaps of barramundi! I'm going to get a big one!'

'Where there's barra, there's crocs,' Xavier says. 'Tom, you shouldn't go out there. It's not fair to tempt that crocodile.'

'There's no crocodiles,' Tom says, annoyed. 'Anyway, Jack can watch the water for me.'

'What?' Jack's eyes are wide with shock.

'When a croc is going to attack,' Tom tells him, 'he breathes out. You'll see the bubbles. All you have to do is watch the water for me. When you see the bubbles, yell out, and I'll jump up there.' Tom points up to the higher branches.

'Are you sure they always make bubbles?' Jack asks.

'Yes!' Tom yells. 'Nanna Clara even told me.'

Jack looks at Xavier to ask if it's true, but Xavier shrugs his shoulders and turns away.

If I was a croc, Jack thinks, *I'd just jump and grab him – like they do when they catch birds. I wouldn't come up slowly, breathing, making bubbles for everyone to see.*

But he knows that if he keeps arguing, Tom will yell at him. So he just gets behind a big log near the edge of the creek and starts watching the water for crocodile bubbles.

Out on the tree trunk, Tom gets the beautiful orange-and-yellow lure

out from under his hat and hooks it
onto his hand line.

He spins the lure round and round
his head, slowly at first, then faster
and faster, and . . . tosses it. The lure

flies out, pulling the line off the reel with a whirr, and plops far out in the deep water.

That was a good cast, Jack thinks, watching Tom as he pulls the line back through the water, fast and slow, jerking it this way and that, so it swims like a real fish. *Tom is a real good fisherman.*

Xavier moves in behind the log with Jack and baits up his line.

'Get us a long stick, Jack, while I cut up the bait,' he says. He cuts the meat into little pieces with his pocket-knife. 'This is the best time of the year to catch perch,' he tells Jack. 'When the speargrass seeds are falling, the little fish are really fat and ready to eat.' He slips the meat onto the hooks and makes a rod with the stick to hold the line away from the water's edge. Straight away little fish start nibbling the meat.

'The little fish pinch the bait,' Xavier says, smiling. 'But the big fish are greedy. They don't want the little fish to get all the tucker. They come and grab the meat and swallow the hook! You watch.'

Jack watches Xavier's line. *Nibble, nibble.* The line jerks in the water. *Nibble, nibble.* It jiggles the stick up and down. Then a bigger fish bites the meat, pulling the stick down hard.

'Black bream,' Xavier whispers.

The black bream sucks the meat into its mouth and spits it out.

Xavier holds the stick rod carefully. Next time he feels the fish suck the bait into its mouth, he jerks the line quickly, hooking the fish through the lip and pulling it up, flapping, onto the bank.

'Yaaah!' Jack yells. 'We got a fish!' Then he remembers he's meant to be watching the water for crocodile bubbles. Quickly he looks back at Tom. *Don't get distracted*, he tells himself. *If Tom gets eaten by a crocodile, it will be your fault!*

Xavier cuts the black bream's neck and puts it safely behind the log. As

soon as the line is back in the water
again, another fish is nibbling. This
time Xavier catches two fish – one
on each hook. Then another. Fish are
flapping around at their feet. Jack has

to get a stick and skewer the fish onto it, through the gill-hole and out the mouth, so the fishes' heads sit on each other, their tails sticking out like a fan.

Chapter Three

Out on the log, Tom hasn't had a bite yet.

'You watching for crocs, Jack?' he yells, annoyed.

'Yeah,' Jack answers. Guiltily he takes his eyes off the stick full of fish and looks back at the water near Tom.

'Come on, big barra,' Tom says. 'Come on, take the lure!'

Next minute, SNAP!

'Yes!' Tom yells. The fishing line races out. It's heavy line, so it won't break, but Tom has to let it run because it is slipping through his hand so fast it's cutting deep into his fingers.

'Big one!' he yells.

Xavier looks up. 'Yeah, right!' Tom always reckons he's got the biggest fish.

The fish jumps up into the air, sparkling silver.

'Unreal!' Xavier and Jack shout together.

Xavier reels in his line quickly so it won't get tangled up with Tom's fish. 'Let him run, Tom!'

'Don't let him go too far,' Jack yells.

'I can't hold him. Bring me a stick to help me hold him!' Tom shouts.

Jack looks at Xavier. 'Who, me?' his

eyes say. 'I'm not going out there!'

But Xavier is already grabbing a
stick off the ground and testing it for
strength. He starts to run out to Tom
along the tree trunk, then he stops and

stares at the water. Jack can see that Xavier doesn't want to go out on that tree trunk where a croc could grab him any time.

But then the fish jumps again and Tom shouts, 'Quick, Xavier, come and grab the reel! I'm going to lose him. I need a stick. Xavier! What are you doing?'

And Xavier runs over the fallen tree, yelling, 'Jack, watch that water for crocs.'

No way! Jack thinks. *Now they're both going to get eaten by a crocodile and it'll be all my fault. It's not fair! I keep getting distracted.*

He forces himself to watch the

water, but already his eyes are hurting from looking so hard for bubbles without blinking. *Please don't let there be a croc*, he wishes. *Please. Please. Please!*

Xavier gives Tom the stick, grabs the hand line, and climbs up into the branches, where he is safe from crocodiles. 'You watching for crocs, Jack?' he says.

'Yeah!'

With the line wrapped around the stick now, Tom can stop the big silver fish running. It jumps again, twisting and turning, trying to get the lure out of its mouth, sending drops of water sparkling into the air.

'He's huge!' Jack yells, excited.

Tom turns around to look at him, smiling. He pulls the line in, wrapping it around the stick with each pull to keep it tight. Up the fish goes again into the air, and back it flops into the water.

'No, don't jump any more,' Tom tells the fish. They have all seen fish jump and spit the lure out in mid air, the line falling slack into the water.

Jack crosses his fingers and holds them in front of his mouth for luck. 'Please don't let it spit,' he prays. 'Please don't let it spit the lure out.'

Then Tom's line goes slack.

'NO!' Tom yells. He pulls the line in as fast as he can, hand over hand, not

caring if it lands in tangles around
his feet.

'Did he spit it out?' Jack yells.

'Nah, he's hooked proper,' Tom says.

'They can still spit it out,' Xavier tells him.

'He didn't!' Tom says, trying to believe it.

Tom pulls, and the line keeps coming and coming as if there is no fish on it.

Jack's heart sinks. *It's not fair. That was the best fish ever!*

Then, just when the line is coming out of the water right by Tom's feet, just when they are all expecting the spat-out lure to pop up, the line gets tighter. 'Hey, he's still on,' Tom yells. 'Yes! I've still got him.'

'Yaaah!' Jack screams, excited. 'Where is he?'

'Under there.' Tom points down under the fallen tree.

'Is he snagged?'

'Yeah.' Tom pulls the line to feel. 'He's gone around something – but it's moving. It must be just a little branch.'

'Pull it hard,' Jack says, impatient to see the fish again.

'No, I might break the line or rip the lure out his mouth.'

'Let him sit,' Xavier says. 'He might come out by himself.'

Chapter Four

They wait and wait.

Watching Tom standing there on the tree trunk, right out in the middle of the water, makes Jack's stomach curl with worry. *A croc could snatch him off that branch without even jumping. Why doesn't he get up in the branches with Xavier?* But Jack can't tell Tom what to do. Tom is his big brother. And anyway, if Jack starts going on about the crocodile again, Tom will only tease him and call him a scaredy little sooky boy. So Jack just keeps his fingers

crossed for luck and keeps watching
the water.

'Big fish, hey?' Tom says, looking at
Xavier and over at Jack on the bank

for confirmation. 'You mob saw it.
A metre long, I reckon.'

'Yeah,' Xavier agrees. Then, leaning forward, he says. 'Hey, Tom! You should come up here. I can see right down deep. I think I can see the lure!'

'Really?' Tom quickly climbs up and settles himself on one of the tree branches high above the water. 'Where?'

'There.' Xavier points to where they can just make out the orange-and-yellow lure beneath the murky water, a little patch of brightness.

'Can you see the fish too?' Jack asks.

'Nah. The line might be wrapped around a branch so he can't move.'

'Just wait,' says Xavier. 'He might swim around and get off.'

Jack stays in his place behind the log. His legs are going numb from crouching. His eyes are getting sleepy from waiting and watching – waiting for the fish, watching for crocodile bubbles.

Then he sees a wallaby moving through the bush. The boys are so quiet that the wallaby doesn't even know they're there. She's only a metre away. Jack looks up at Tom and Xavier without moving his head to smile at them about the wallaby. To share the joke that she doesn't know they're there. But Xavier and Tom are looking at the water.

The wallaby has a joey in her pouch. Jack can see the pouch hanging heavy

in front of her. It's a big joey. As the wallaby moves to the water's edge, she sniffs the air, searching for danger. Her ears move back and forth, listening for any sound. The whiskers around her nose twitch. Her big brown eyes are frightened.

She knows there are crocs around, Jack thinks. *But she has to drink. She needs lots of water to make milk for her joey. I bet she's hoping the crocs are down on the sandbar, using the sun to keep them warm. If the crocs are down there, she'll be safe. But if they aren't, she might be in big trouble.*

Chapter Five

Stop watching the wallaby, Jack tells himself. He drags his eyes back to watch the water for bubbles. Tom and Xavier are staring at the water, trying to see the fish. The wind is whistling in the trees and rushing up the creek, lifting the surface of the water into shimmering ripples. They sparkle in the sunlight.

Just then the wind dies down. The little ripples smooth out. The sun goes behind a cloud, so there's no light reflecting off the water.

Tom jerks forward. He's seen something. He touches Xavier quietly and points, to tell him he can see a shape – the fish?

And the shape moves.

It starts to swim away. The fish shape is connected to a huge body, legs, tail.

It's moving toward the bank.

'CROC! Yahhhhh!' Tom screams. 'Jack, look out! Run!'

The wallaby hears Tom yell, and jumps.

The croc lunges, white water splashing into the air.

SNAP! His jaws crunch together where the wallaby was, missing her body, just catching one of her legs and pulling her – *thud!* – smashing to the ground right next to Jack. She kicks and kicks, trying to get away. The croc jerks its head up and down, lifting her into the air.

Jack can hear Tom and Xavier screaming, 'Get away! Run, Jack, run!' But he can't move. He's stuck. The croc is huge! Right there. Its mouth is

clamped on the skinny little wallaby leg. He wants to run, but his brain has stopped.

Then time stops.

The croc is still. He has the wallaby by one leg. He might lose her if he's not careful.

The wallaby is also still. She knows the only chance she and her baby have is to play dead. The croc needs to get a

better grip, and he won't chance it till he thinks she's dead.

The crocodile waits. Then slowly he opens his mouth and turns his head sideways.

Instantly the wallaby jumps, her good leg finds the ground, and she bounces out of reach.

The croc lunges again. This time his aim is perfect. His jaws close tightly around the wallaby's hindquarters. She's trapped.

The croc twists his body from side to side, smashing the wallaby onto the ground.

Something flings off her body, flies through the air and lands in the leaves.

Thud! Thud! The croc smashes and smashes.

Then he stops, waits a moment.

Holding his head up high, so the wallaby's body hangs limp from his jaws, he slips back into the creek. The murky water smooths over.

Silence.

No birds screeching.

No cockatoos.

Nothing.

Chapter Six

Tom and Xavier are shaking with panic. They saw the splash, and water going everywhere. At first they thought it was Jack – that the croc had got Jack! But it's okay. It was only a wallaby. Jack is still there behind the log, just as he was. He hasn't moved a centimetre.

If the ground wasn't all wet from the splash, if there wasn't a huge crocodile slide smooth in the clay where the croc slipped back into the water, you'd think nothing had happened.

'You all right, Jack?' Xavier yells.

'You right?'

Jack doesn't answer.

'Jack? Jack!'

Xavier looks at Tom, really worried. 'We got to help him.'

'What about the croc?'

'He'll be right now. He's got the wallaby. He's not going to attack us now.'

'What about the lure?' Tom says. 'Dad's gonna kill me if he finds out I took his lure.'

Xavier glares at Tom. 'Don't worry about yourself,' he says, his voice angry. 'Worry about your brother.' And he runs across the tree trunk to Jack.

'Jack,' he says, grabbing him by the arm.

Jack doesn't move. He is absolutely still, just sitting and staring.

'This is bad,' Xavier says. 'Nanna Clara told me stories about this. She said some people who get a big fright can die inside.' He waves his hand in front of Jack's face. 'Jack, listen to me!'

Jack doesn't blink, doesn't move.

'Come on, Jack,' Xavier says. 'I'm taking you to Nanna Clara.' He stands Jack up, lifts him onto his back and starts to run back down to where Nanna Clara mob were sitting on the bank. *Gotta hold him close,* he thinks. *Keep him warm. In contact.*

Tom cuts the fishing line, ties it up to one of the higher branches on the fallen tree, and runs back across the

41

tree to the bank. He picks up the hand line and the stick full of fish. With one last look at where his big fish is, he takes off after Xavier.

Jack is little, but he's really heavy. He's not hanging on. He's like a dead weight. Xavier's hands keep slipping out from under Jack's legs. He has to keep stopping, jumping to hitch him up higher, and then running again.

When he gets closer to the sandbar, he is so out of breath he has to stop. He breathes heavily for ages before he can yell, 'Nanna! Nanna! Nanna Clara!'

'Aye,' her voice answers from up

the bank. Xavier knows she must be
sitting by the fire in the creek-bank
camp.

He runs into the camp, turns
around and squats to get Jack off his

back. Jack sits down on the ground next to Nanna Clara, quiet and still.

'Whatkind?' Nanna Clara passes her baby grandchild to Xavier's cousin, Mareeta. 'Hold him, good girl,' she says. Then she looks at Xavier. *What happened?* her eyes ask him.

Xavier is bent over, his hands on his knees, breathing heavily. He doesn't want to tell Nanna Clara about Tom going out on the fallen tree in the middle of the creek when he knows there could be crocs around. It's not up to him to tell on Tom and get him into trouble. And anyway, it's not Xavier's story to tell. Tom has to tell that story himself.

The baby starts to cry. Xavier quickly takes him from Mareeta and walks away with him so Nanna Clara can't ask him any more questions. 'Look there,' he says to the baby. 'Look at the paperbark flower.'

Nanna Clara pulls Jack onto her legs. His body is shivering. His face is very still. He doesn't look at her.

'Make that billy,' Nanna Clara tells Mareeta.

Mareeta heaps up the fire to make the billy hot.

Tom comes running up the track. 'Biggest crocodile, Nanna Clara!' he yells. 'Jumped out of the water for a wallaby! Scared the hell out of Jack!

Biggest crocodile you've ever seen!'
He stretches out his arms to show
how huge it was. 'This wide across the
head!'

Xavier's grandad comes up the bank
with a fish in each hand. 'What's the
matter?' he asks.

'Biggest crocodile,' Tom says. 'Jump.
Water. Splash white water.' His words
tumble over each other, trying to tell.

'Where?'

'I'll show you,' Tom says, dropping
Xavier's fish and the hand lines down
beside the fire.

'Make that tea first. Put plenty
sugar inside,' Nanna Clara tells him.

Tom makes the tea and pours a cup

for Nanna Clara. He watches her face
to see how many sugars to put in. She
lets him put in five before she nods,
That's enough.

'Come on,' Tom calls Xavier, and

they start back up the creek to show
Grandad where it all happened.

'I'm coming too,' Mareeta calls.

The baby has stopped crying now
and Xavier swings him up onto his
shoulder.

They go, leaving Jack and Nanna
Clara still sitting by the fire.

Chapter Seven

The voices slowly fade away to quiet.
Around the camp, small birds move in
the treetops. The water murmurs in
the creek.

'Jack?' Nanna Clara says. 'Jack?'

Silence.

She pulls him tightly onto her
lap and starts to rock him. 'You good
boy. You good boy,' she says, rocking
him hard, backwards and forwards,
backwards and forwards, twisting her
body right around each time. 'You good
boy. You good boy.'

Jack's eyes are open, and they watch the trees slip from side to side, whirring into lines of green and brown. They don't register in his mind as trees. They're just lines. His mind is not thinking. His body is soft inside, dark like a cave, but empty and foggy. He could stay in there forever, but then the rocking gets harder and harder, jerking his head. He doesn't like it. He feels his body rocking inside itself. He feels his brain inside his head and the muscles in his neck as his body moves back and forth, twisting and jerking.

He wants to stop, but he can't. The rocking is making him move.

He doesn't want to move. He tries
to stop, to make himself stiff to fight
against it.

And it stops – Nanna Clara stops.

The world comes into focus. The trees, the fire, the fish.

'Drink.' Nanna Clara makes him drink tea. It's sweet and black and warm. Warm on his hands, warm inside his belly.

Then Nanna Clara pulls him back tight against her body and starts singing in Mayali language, her own mother's language.

It's a strange song. Mournful. It calls up all the fear inside him. His body shudders. He sees the crocodile. He tries not to look. He tries to hold the image down, but it just comes right out of the water, mouth open, orange inside, water splashing up like an explosion around it; huge teeth crunching on the wallaby's back, smash, smashing the wallaby's head against the ground.

Nanna Clara keeps singing and the images float past.

'There were no bubbles!' Jack says slowly.

The song pulls the feelings and the words from him.

'He just jumped up. No bubbles. Just still water. I was watching. I was!'

'Sometime they don't make bubble,' Nanna Clara says, holding him tight.

'Tom said they always make bubbles.'

'It might be old clever one, that

crocodile. Maybe he knew you were watching for him. Maybe he held his breath.'

'I was watching,' Jack says, angry tears running down his face. 'He didn't make bubbles. Really! It's not my fault!'

'You're a good boy, you're a good boy,' Nanna Clara says, rocking him softly.

Jack cries, remembering the croc smell, his teeth, the scared little wallaby caught in the croc's jaws, and as the tears flow down his face they take his fear and he relaxes down into Nanna Clara's lap. His chest loosens up and he breathes in that lovely smell of Nanna Clara, the smell of cooking fires and bush food.

He is safe. His body is tingling and
his legs are still a bit wobbly, but he
feels safe.

Nanna Clara sings softly for him,
holding him close. Then she says,

'They very smart, them old crocodile. They can even get *Gurdangyi*, sometimes, even though he is a law man who knows all the magic and ceremony. A clever old crocodile can still catch that *Gurdangyi*.'

Jack looks up at her. 'True?'

'True God,' she says, and she smiles, holding his face tight against her chest, roughly shaking him. 'And sometimes,' she tells him, her face serious, 'when that crocodile scares someone really properly – he can give them some spirit.'

'Hey?' Jack asks in disbelief.

'That's right!'

'Like what?'

'Like maybe that person might subbie all crocodiles then. He might understand them, might know how they are thinking.'

'True?'

'True story.'

'Wow!' Jack smiles and leans back onto Nanna Clara's lap.

Her eyes fill with tears as she laughs. Jack is back! He's not hiding inside his head. He's all right. He's still alive.

Chapter Eight

Down the creek Tom and Xavier show Grandad the huge slide down the bank into the water. 'There, see?'

'Look, big slide for that crocodile,' Xavier says, showing the baby the crocodile track sliding into the water.

No one goes near the water. There's death in the air.

Everyone stands looking at the slide.

Xavier and Tom don't want to say too much or they'll have to admit they were out on the fallen tree, fishing.

It looks so dangerous now. None of
them would go out there!

Then there's a movement in some
leaves beside Tom's foot. He jumps
with fright, thinking it might be
a snake.

It's a little joey.

Everyone's laughing at Tom because he got a fright.

The joey is lying in the leaves, its big eyes wide open, its long legs shivering. It's covered with soft down, the pink skin shining through.

'Look out, Tom,' Xavier says. 'Big crocodile!'

'Shuddup!' Tom says, picking the little joey up. There are ants all over it, biting into its skin. He holds it up to show them, and its little legs jerk as if it's trying to get away.

'Give it here,' Mareeta says. 'Don't be cruel, Tom.'

'No! It's mine. I found it.'

'It's cold!'

'I know!' He wipes the ants off
and wraps it in his shirt, close to his
skin. *Wicked*, he thinks. *I'll be able to
take it to school. Everyone will want to look.
I'll make a little pouch and carry it around
all day.*

'Where'd it come from?' Mareeta
asks.

'From that wallaby. They can throw
their baby away when they get chased,'
Tom says.

'Gammon!' Mareeta says, telling
him it's not true.

'It is so true,' Tom says. 'Sometimes
when dingoes chase wallabies and they
get real tired, they chuck their baby

in the bush and come back for it later. That's right, aye Grandad?'

Grandad nods. He's looking out over the swollen creek. 'How come there's fishing line there?' he asks.

'Where?' Tom says innocently.

'There.' Grandad points to where Tom's line is tied up in the branch of the tree.

Tom and Xavier go silent.

Grandad turns to look at them. 'Were you fishing there?'

Silence.

Grandad waits, looking at Tom.

Tom nods his head.

Xavier looks at the ground.

'Why is that line there?' Grandad asks.

'I caught a big fish. A huge
barramundi,' Tom says.

Grandad looks at him, not believing.

'A big one!' Tom says. 'More than
a metre long!'

'Xavier?'

Xavier looks up. 'He's snagged there.'

'Properly?'

Xavier nods.

Grandad looks at the water for a long time. He's searching for the crocodile.

Every croc has his own territory. When he catches something, he doesn't eat it straight away. He stashes it somewhere, guards it, and eats it when the flesh is soft. This croc won't be hunting again today, but he'll attack anyone if he thinks they might try and steal his food.

'There,' Grandad says.

They all look. 'Where?'

Grandad bends down low and points so all the kids can look along his arm. There on the other side of the creek is a thick tangle of logs and pandanus roots. In the middle is the fawn-coloured fur of the wallaby, just sticking above the surface of the water.

'The crocodile is right there,' Grandad says. 'He's watching us.'

The kids stare at the water, looking.

'There,' Grandad says again.

And they see him. The crocodile, just his eyes and nose out of the water, floating lazily in the sun, watching them. Looking like a piece of wood floating on the current.

'You mob want to get your fish?' Grandad says, staring at Tom and Xavier really hard.

Both boys shake their heads.

Tom feels sick in the guts. *That croc was there all the time. All the time I was standing out there on the fallen tree. I didn't even look around to check.*

He holds the little joey tight to stop his belly churning up with shame and fear.

Chapter Nine

They walk back to Nanna Clara.

Jack is sitting quietly on her lap, gazing at the campfire.

'These mob been fishing out on that water,' Grandad says. 'They been tempting that crocodile.'

Nanna Clara looks fiercely at Xavier.

'Not Xavier,' Tom says. 'Just me. Xavier was on the bank.'

Nanna Clara shakes her head. 'You should have told him not to go there,' she says to Xavier.

'I did!' Xavier says. 'He didn't listen to me.'

Nanna Clara looks fiercely at Tom, then shakes her head again – so ashamed.

Tom sits down by the fire, feeling really stupid. He thought it was going to be the best fishing trip ever. And it would have been if he'd got that big barramundi. But now it's all gone wrong. *Jack's all tongue-tied*, he thinks. *Nanna Clara is ashamed of me. Dad's lure is lost. And it's all my fault.*

Then the little joey kicks. Tom opens his shirt. 'Hey,' he says. 'Look what I found.'

Jack's eyes light up. 'A joey!'

Tom hands it to him.

'Can I have him?'

'Yeah.'

'Nanna Clara, look!' Jack says.

Nanna Clara touches the little joey. *'Ahnan,'* she says. 'Too cute! Hold him close up. Keep him warm.'

Xavier is so happy Jack's talking again that he teases him. 'Look out, Jack, biggest crocodile coming.'

'I can subbie crocodile now,' Jack says, proud.

'What, you reckon you Crocodile Jack now?' Xavier says. He laughs, pretending to bite Jack. 'Look out, crocodile gonna get you!'

Jack just laughs. 'Get lost, Xavier.'

'Why didn't he take us, that big
crocodile?' Tom asks Nanna Clara.
'He was right there. He could have
got Jack. How come he just went for
that wallaby?'

Nanna Clara thinks for a long time. Finally she says, 'It might be that crocodile is your totem,' she says. 'The same as Xavier.'

'Crocodile Jack! I told you,' Xavier says, trying to make everyone laugh.

But Nanna Clara keeps her face serious, looking first at Tom and then at Jack to get their attention. Then she says, 'If you have a crocodile totem, you have to be responsible for him. You can't make him hungry. You can't tempt him, make him want to eat you. You can't eat him, you subbie? You can't eat crocodile. And he can't eat you.'

Later, when Tom and Jack are walking

home, Jack says, 'We got a crocodile totem, Tom. Too good.'

'Yeah,' Tom says. 'But you and me are going to be in big trouble when Dad finds out his lure is missing.'

'Me?' Jack asks.

'Well, I didn't climb through the shed window and steal the lure,' Tom says.

'But you told me to.'

Tom shrugs his shoulders. 'You didn't have to do it,' he says.

That night Jack dreams about the lure. In a few weeks' time, when the creek has gone down, he imagines Dad getting ready to go fishing.

He gets out his fishing rods and tackle box. He opens his tackle box and finds the empty container. His orange-and-yellow Vibra Tail is gone. Dad turns and looks at Jack, his face angry. 'Did you steal my lure?'

Jack wakes up sweating. In the bed next to him he can hear Tom tossing and turning with worry too.

Crossing his arms and his legs for luck, Jack begs the crocodile, *Please, if you are my totem, please don't touch the fish. Please don't break the line and take the fish and the lure. Leave it there so we can get the lure back and not get into trouble.*

Chapter Ten

The next morning, when it's still dark, Jack and Tom are awake. 'We've got to get Dad's lure back,' Tom says.

'How?' Jack answers. 'I'm not going near that tree till that croc has gone back to sea.'

'Yeah, but the croc won't go till the creek is down. That's when Dad will go fishing.'

They lie on their beds, thinking in silence for ages. Then Jack says, 'How can you tell when a croc has gone back to sea?'

'Don't know. Let's go ask Nanna Clara.'

They run down the road to Xavier's house. The air is warm, and the horizon glows orange in the early morning sky.

Nanna Clara is already up. She's outside, making billy tea on a fire.

'Nanna Clara,' Jack says, 'how do you know when the crocodiles are gone?'

'You want to go fishing again?' Nanna Clara asks them, her eyes wide, dark and angry. She grabs Jack by the arm. 'You going fishing?'

'No!' Jack and Tom both answer.

'But we lost Dad's lure,' Tom says. 'I caught this big barramundi and he got snagged and the lure is still there, caught on the tree. If Dad finds out we took his lure, we'll be in the biggest trouble.'

Nanna Clara looks at them, thinking about what to say, sipping her tea and looking them right in the eye. 'You have to go and look at the water every day. Look and see where the crocodile is, every day. You walk. Not near the water! Up high on the bank. You sneak quietly and look where he is lying in the sun, getting warm. Then one day he's gone. Then another day he's gone. Then he's gone back to the sea.

'When the sun is up there,' she says,

pointing to where the sun will be at
about ten o'clock. 'Come back then, and
I will take you and show you.'

Later in the morning Xavier, Tom and
Jack follow Nanna Clara down to the
sandbar to look for the crocodile.

They walk up the creek, staying right up high on the bank and walking carefully so they don't make a noise in the dry leaves. They look down wherever they see a patch of sun on the muddy river bank.

But there's nothing there. No crocodile staying as still as a rock, his skin covered with brown mud, eyes half closed with pleasure as he soaks up the sun.

'He's gone already,' Tom says.

'No! I know where he is,' Jack says. And he runs further down the creek.

Sure enough, there he is. The huge crocodile is up on the bank not far from the fallen tree, lying in the sun, his mouth open, his body spread out and still.

After that, the strangest thing happens.

Each day, when Xavier, Tom and Jack go down to the creek to find the crocodile, no matter where the croc is, Jack always finds him. He just knows where to look.

'Just ask Crocodile Jack,' Xavier reckons.

When they tell Nanna Clara, she laughs and nods her head as if to say, 'I told you that might happen.'

And each day, as soon as they know where the crocodile is, the boys go down and check to make sure the

fishing line is still hanging from the
tree with the fish and the lure below.

Weeks go by. The creek water clears
and slows, grass and ferns start

growing on the muddy banks. But still the crocodile stays in the creek.

One night, at dinner, Dad says, 'Got to get the fishing tackle sorted. Nearly time to go fishing.'

'Wha – ?' Jack says, panicking.

Tom freezes, the fork halfway to his mouth, his eyes wide.

'What's the matter with you boys?' Dad asks. 'I thought you'd be excited to go fishing.'

'Yeah, we are, but . . .' Tom says.

Jack keeps his eyes on his plate, forcing himself to chew and swallow.

The next day Jack and Tom rush down to check on the croc. But they can't find him anywhere. He's not on the sandbar. He's not floating on the water, just his eyes and nose above the surface. He's not as still as a log on the bank, waiting. He's not snuggled into the muddy bank. He's gone.

They run back to Nanna Clara.

'The croc's gone!' Jack yells.

'Wait now,' she tells them. 'Look tomorrow,' she lifts one finger. 'If you can't find him, we will look the next day,' showing two fingers. 'Then we will know if he is really gone.'

The next day lasts forever. Tom and Jack escape from home early, not wanting to hang around in case Dad mentions going fishing again.

They spend all day with Xavier, walking along the river looking for the crocodile. There's no sign of him anywhere.

'He's really gone,' Tom tells Nanna Clara.

'Nomore humbug me,' she tells him, closing her eyes and putting her hand up to tell him not to hassle her. 'Sometimes those old crocodiles will stay quiet and rest before they go back to the sea. You wait now. Tomorrow we will look.'

Next morning Jack and Tom are awake at first light. 'Let's go and check,' Jack says.

'It's dark, little brother. The sun isn't even up yet,' Tom tells him. 'Crocs don't come out of the water till the sun is up.'

But they can't go back to sleep, so they run down the road to Xavier's place. They have tea and toast with Nanna Clara and hang around impatiently, kicking a football with Xavier and playing chasings with the little kids.

As soon as the sun is high and warm, they ask, 'Nanna, can we go now?'

'Let me see,' she says, standing up and grabbing her stick and her dilly bag.

Nanna Clara looks everywhere. She stops and sniffs the air for the smell

of the croc. She pokes her stick in the
sand, looking for recent tracks, feeling
if the sand is warm from his body. Then
she nods. 'He's gone all right,' she says.

'Can we get the lure now?' Tom asks.

She laughs and shakes her head.
'Yes, you can go!'

The boys run up the creek. The fallen tree is right up above the water now.

Tom walks out along the trunk, grabs the line, and pulls it up.

The lure comes up first, covered with mud.

Then the fish's head – it's huge!

And the body, a skeleton, just little bits of sinew holding it together.

'That's gotta be the biggest fish anyone's caught,' Tom says, standing up, holding the fish skeleton above the water.

Xavier shakes his head in disbelief.

'What a waste!' Tom says, his throat all thick with sadness. 'It's the biggest

fish anyone has ever caught, and
we can't show anyone.'

'I know!' Jack says. 'Let's hang it
in a tree near the shop and make
everyone jealous. They won't know
it's us.'

'Good idea!' Tom and Xavier say
together.

They scrub the orange-and-yellow
Vibra Tail with sand to make it clean
and shiny again. Then, as soon as they
get home, Jack climbs through the
shed window and puts it back in Dad's
tackle box.

That evening, after everyone else
has gone to bed, the three boys sneak
out and run down the road. They tie

the fish skeleton to a high branch in one of the big gum trees near the shop. Jack stands on Xavier's shoulders, and Tom hands the fish skeleton up to him.

The next day everyone's stopping and looking and saying, 'Who caught that fish? Look at the size of it!'

A tourist even takes a photo.

And the boys are sitting in the shade nearby, Xavier, Tom and Crocodile Jack, watching and smiling.

From Leonie Norrington

When I was growing up, I lived with my family (there were nine of us kids) in a remote community in the Northern Territory. We were real bush kids, and we grew up among Aboriginal people who lived in the traditional way.
My big brothers did lots of things together and would never let me go with them.
They thought I was a *girl*.
I wrote this story to show that all people, no matter how young or little they are, can be clever and good to have in your gang.

From Terry Denton

I grew up in the city with a street full of brothers and friends. We played football and cricket, made cubbies and, in summer, we swam in the river. One day a dead cow floated by our swimming hole, but apart from that nothing much ever happened.
A river full of crocodiles might have made my life more exciting. Or shorter.

Haggis McGregor is about
to have the time of
his . . . death!

Why is it so hard
being a Viking warrior?

Will Kasem be able
to keep his promise
to the elephant?

Why is it that dads
have no shame?
Oh, the embarrassment!